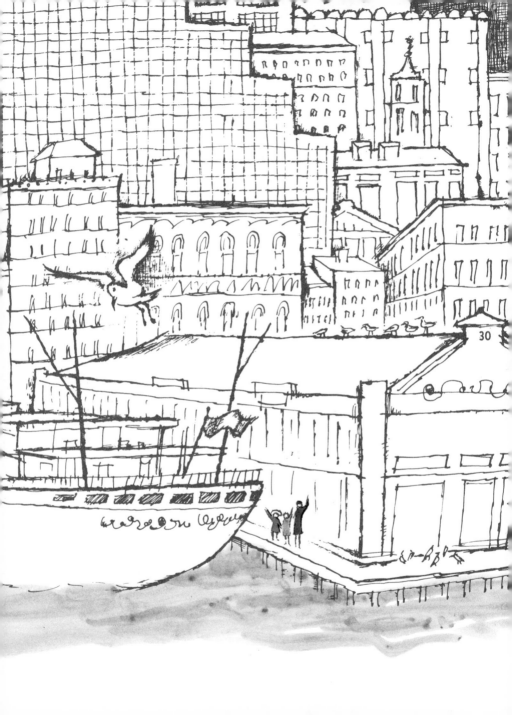

Noisy Nancy and Nick

Noisy Nancy and Nick

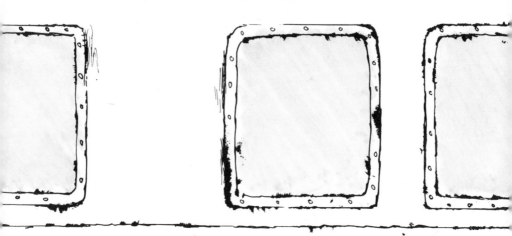

by Lou Ann Gaeddert
illustrated by Gioia Fiammenghi

Doubleday & Co., Inc., Garden City, New York

ISBN: 0-385-07922-2 TRADE
0-385-01542-9 PREBOUND
Library of Congress Catalog Card Number 70-79385
9   8   7   6   5   4   3

For my daughter Martha

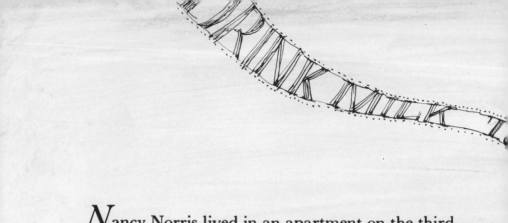

*N*ancy Norris lived in an apartment on the third floor of a tall building. She liked noise.

She played elephant with cake pans for great clattering feet.

She swung between two chairs and screeched like a monkey.

She rattled paper and thumped clay. She
marched and sang. She clomped and hopped

Mrs. Muffle lived in an apartment just below the Norris family. She didn't like noise. On days when Nancy's games were very loud, Mrs. Muffle would bang on her ceiling with a broom handle. Nancy would hear the bang and know that it was time to be quiet.

One rainy afternoon, when Nancy was slithering across the floor, practicing her seal barks, she heard a loud ringing noise in the hall. She ran to the door and looked out.

A boy was walking up the stairs hitting every iron post of the railing with a bat. Nancy got her stick horse and galloped up the stairs after the boy, hitting the posts with the end of the stick.

"Oh no, children," called Nancy's mother.
"You can't do that. You'll disturb everybody in
the building."

Nancy and the boy sat down on the stairs and stared at one another.

"You can't do anything in an apartment," the boy said at last. "I hate the city."

Nancy introduced herself. The boy said his name was Nick. He had just moved into an apartment on the fourth floor. He came from a small town in Ohio.

"We had our own house and yard with grass to roll on and trees to climb," he said. "I even had my own garden."

"Do you want to see my marigolds?" Nancy asked.

Nick nodded, and the children went to Nancy's room to look at the flowerpot on her window sill.

"They're pretty," said Nick, "but that's not much of a garden. I grew peas and beans and tomatoes."

Nancy and Nick built a huge tower with Nancy's blocks. They sat and looked at it for a while. Then Nancy got her dump truck and zoomed it into the base of the tower. Blocks crashed to the floor.

"Let's do it again," shouted Nick.

They were building a new tower when they heard a bang on the floor.

"What's that?" asked Nick.

"That's the lady downstairs," explained Nancy. "We're too noisy. We can't knock our tower down this time."

"I'd better go upstairs," whispered Nick as he tiptoed to the door. "I wish I could go home and play with my friends in Ohio. We didn't have to be quiet there."

Nick turned and ran up the stairs, but Nancy saw that there were tears in his eyes.

Nancy went back to her room and climbed on
the head of her bed. She pretended she was sitting
in a tree.

Then she flopped down on the mattress.

During dinner, Nancy told her mother and
father about Nick and how he had cried.

"He says he hates the city," said Nancy.

"Maybe you could help him like it," Daddy sug-
gested. "What do you think he'd like in the city?"

Nancy thought for a minute. "You know what *I'd* like? I'd like the big boats. Nick would like them too. Let's go down to the docks tomorrow."

Father looked in the paper and said that an ocean liner was sailing for Italy in the morning.

Nancy's mother went to ask Nick's mother if he could go with them to see it.

The next morning
the two children and
Mrs. Norris went down
to the pier.
A band was playing
on the huge, white ship.

They clattered up all the stairs
on to the top deck

and down all the stairs to the bottom deck.

They ran down the long halls.

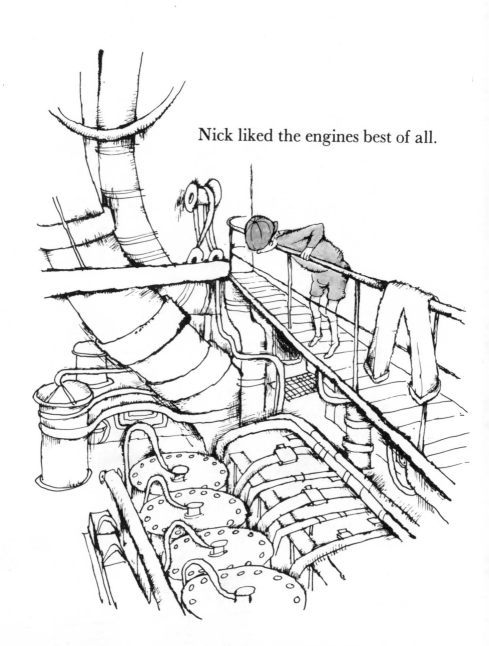

Nick liked the engines best of all.

They were playing tag around the life boats when a new sound, a long, loud blast, boomed over their heads.

"That's the ship's whistle," Mother explained. "It means that it is time for visitors to leave."

As they walked off the ship,
an officer in a white uniform said
"Arrivederci" to the children.
"That means 'good-by' in Italian,"
Mother said.
Nick and Nancy stood at the bottom
of the gangplank and shouted
"ARRIVEDERCI" to the people
above them on the ship.

Mother and the children sat on a bench and watched the ship get ready to sail to Italy. When a man came by with a cart selling pizzas, they bought their lunch from him.

"This is more fun than eating lunch in a drug-store," Nick said.

At last the little tugs had pushed the huge ship out into the river and down toward the ocean.

Mother asked Nancy to hail a taxi. Nancy stood on the curb and held out her hand, shouting, "Cab." Nick shouted too. A taxi stopped and took them to a large department store.

"How do you get on that?" Nick asked, pointing to the escalator.

Nancy stepped on and was halfway up to the second floor when she looked back and saw Mother helping Nick get on.

"Jump when you get to the top," Nancy called to Nick.

Nancy stepped off and waited for Nick.

He reached the top and made a mighty leap. He flew through the air, knocking a pile of towels off a counter. People gathered around him to see if he was hurt.

"That was fun," he said with a laugh. "Let's go up to the next floor."

Mother and the children folded the towels and put them back. They rode escalators all the way to the top floor toy department. They looked at the toys and rode escalators all the way down to the basement. Then they spun themselves through revolving doors.

"This is a subway station," Nancy explained. She led Nick and her mother to the very end of the platform so that they could be in the first car.

When the train came roaring into the station, Nancy and Nick ran to the front window. The subway jerked forward, then it gathered speed and swayed from side to side through a long dark tunnel.

"What a tippy train!" Nick exclaimed as he spread his feet and tried to stand without holding on. When they pulled into the next station, he gasped. "Look," he shouted. "They sell doughnuts way down here."

"Sure," said Nancy. "There are all kinds of stores in the subway stations. It's like a city under the city."

They got off at the stop nearest home and
climbed the stairs to the street. Mother said they
had to buy meat for dinner.

"Where's the supermarket?" Nick asked.

"We don't have big supermarkets with huge parking lots like the one you went to in Ohio," Mother explained. "Today I'm just going to the butcher shop."

"Big supermarkets are better," Nick announced.

The butcher greeted Nancy and her mother. He gave each child a slice of baloney. Then he cut and wrapped the lamb chops for Nancy's dinner.

Nancy ran out of the shop.
Nick ran after her.

He saw her up ahead and then, all of a sudden, she was gone. Nick walked slowly up the street, looking in all of the shops. He saw a fruit store with bins of vegetables out on the sidewalk.

"Boo," shouted Nancy. She jumped up from be-
hind a bin of potatoes.

Both children laughed. The man in the doorway of the store laughed too.

"You're a clown, Nancy," he said. He broke off a little stem of grapes and handed it to her.

"I can't believe it," said Nick as they walked on toward their apartments. "The city is so big and still the store people know your name and they give you things. The people in our supermarket in Ohio never knew my name, and they never gave me anything."

"Still, small towns must be nice," said Nancy thoughtfully. "I'd like to live in a house where I could make a lot of noise all the time. I'd like to climb trees and plant a real garden. But there are nice things in the city too. There are . . ."

"Ocean liners, and escalators and pizza carts and little stores," interrupted Nick.

"And playgrounds," shouted Nancy. "Come with us tomorrow and see our swings and slides and monkey bars and sandpile."

Nick laughed. "I'll come but don't think you'll show me anything new. Playgrounds are every-place, even in Ohio. I'll bet I can climb faster and higher than you can."

At the door of Nick's apartment, Nick and his mother thanked Nancy and her mother for the nice day.

"Arrivederci," Nick shouted as Nancy and her mother walked down the stairs to their apartment.

"Arrivederci," Nancy called back.
"Shhhh," said Mother.

Gioia Fiammenghi was born in New York City, and attended various art schools in that city. She has illustrated over thirty-four books, both for children and adults, which have been chosen as outstanding in the New York *Times;* the Child Study Association *Book of the Year* for 1963 and 1965; and the Library of Congress *Junior Book List* for 1965.

She lives with her husband, Guido Caputo, and their three young sons in Nice, France. She was included in the 1966 edition of Outstanding Young Women of America.

Lou Ann Gaeddert has had varied experience in the publishing field, working with both books and newspapers, and this is the second book she has written about Noisy Nancy Norris. As the apartment-dwelling mother of two young children, she has chosen a subject with which she is very familiar.

Mrs. Gaeddert is a graduate of the University of Washington. Seattle is her home town, but she and her family now live in Queens, New York.

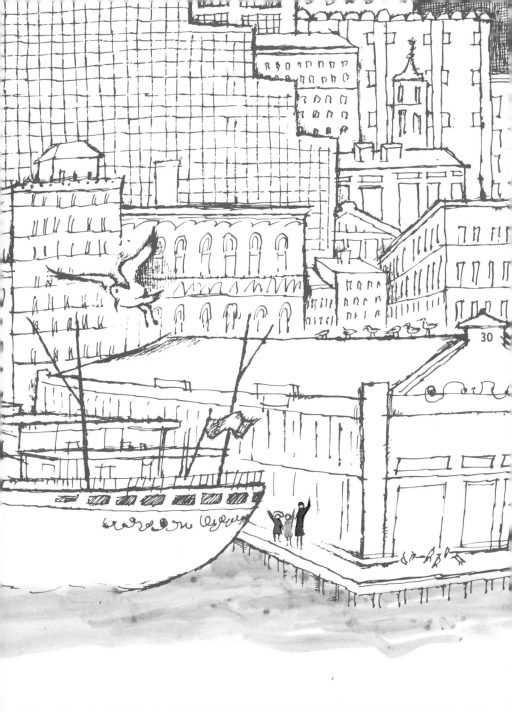